Tortuga

Tortuga

PAUL GERAGHTY

RED FOX

Dark clouds blotted out the sun and the sky
began to rumble. Tortuga took one look, then
tucked into her shell. A big storm was coming.

The wind whipped up the waves and bent the trees. Branches flew in the howling gale and soon whole trunks were ripped from the ground. Tortuga clung to a log, but the storm was so wild she was swept up into the sky.

When light returned, she found herself floating in the ocean. Heavy with eggs and aching with hunger, she drifted for days with nothing but waves and sky as far as the eye could see.

On the fourth day, a lush green island appeared on the horizon. Tortuga's heart quickened. Land had passed her by before, but always out of reach. This time she bobbed slowly through the shallows, quietly hoping the current wouldn't change.

Tortuga's log bumped ashore.
  Startled ghost crabs stopped to watch as the strange new creature scrambled from the surf and across the sand.

At twilight Tortuga began to lay her eggs, but raiding
sea birds swooped down to steal them. Bravely she
stood over her nest, but one after another they came,
quick and fierce, until she couldn't fight anymore.

Exhausted and sad, she moved away. She would have to find another mate, and a safer place to live.

The forest was alive with animals, and food grew everywhere, but Tortuga couldn't find another tortoise.

Perhaps she would have better luck on the mountain
that towered up from the centre of the island.

But steep terrain is no place for a tortoise, and soon
she found herself rolling and tumbling, bouncing and
bumping until she came to a stop on a rocky ledge.
She was upside down and helpless, and the more she
struggled the closer she inched to the edge.

A monitor lizard appeared on the rock and eyed her greedily. Behind her, two more watched and waited. Now she had to stay tucked tightly inside her shell or be eaten. But the sun was baking hot and Tortuga was drying out. In a last frantic bid for freedom, she stretched her legs and flailed about.

At once the lizards pounced . . .

. . . and Tortuga was knocked from the cliff. Down she plunged towards the rocks below.

With a mighty splash she landed in a cool, fresh pool and dragging herself from the water, realised she was on the other side of the island. She found new types of trees and animals, but still no tortoises.

Day after day she searched, and as the weeks passed into months she wondered if she would ever find a mate.

Then rounding a bend one morning, her heart sank.
Before her lay the beach she had landed on so long
ago. She had searched the whole island and still she
was alone.

  For a long time she stood; then very slowly she
trudged away. Tortuga felt like the only tortoise left
in the world.

  Just then, a movement caught her eye. Could it be –

It was! A baby tortoise was hurrying towards her!

And not only one; a whole scramble of tortoises came tumbling out of the brush. Not all of her eggs had been taken. Through her long and lonely search, Tortuga's babies had been thriving by the nest that she had fought so hard to protect.

It wasn't long before they grew up and had families of their own. And now the tortoises are as much a part of the island as the lizards and the birds, the butterflies and the bees that were there when she first scrambled from the sea.

To the Shambollix and Joe Riley & the Four Heads

TORTUGA
A RED FOX BOOK 0 09 948308 4

First published in Great Britain by Hutchinson Children's Books
an imprint of Random House Children's Books

Hutchinson edition published 2000
Red Fox edition published 2001

1 3 5 7 9 10 8 6 4 2

Copyright © Paul Geraghty, 2000

Red Fox Books are published by Random House Children's Books,
61–63 Uxbridge Road, London W5 5SA,
a division of The Random House Group Ltd,
in Australia by Random House Australia (Pty) Ltd,
20 Alfred Street, Milsons Point, Sydney, NSW 2061, Australia,
in New Zealand by Random House New Zealand Ltd,
18 Poland Road, Glenfield, Auckland 10, New Zealand,
and in South Africa by Random House (Pty) Ltd,
Endulini, 5A Jubilee Road, Parktown 2193, South Africa

THE RANDOM HOUSE GROUP Limited Reg. No. 954009

www.kidsatrandomhouse.co.uk
www.paulgeraghty.net

A CIP catalogue record for this book is available from the British Library.

Printed in Hong Kong